W9-ASL-842

May I Visit?

CHARLOTTE ZOLOTOW
May I Visit?

With Illustrations by Erik Blegvad

An Ursula Nordstrom Book

Harper & Row, Publishers
New York, Hagerstown, San Francisco, London

J
Z

For Cres, of course

The big sister
who was married
had just gone back home.

She had come overnight
for a visit
and slept in her old room,

sat in the kitchen
having coffee with their mother.

She had helped to set the table
and talked and talked and talked.

She didn't steam up the bathroom
or spill talcum on the floor

or say, "Oh Mother!"
the way she used to.

It was nice, her being back.

When she went home

the little girl said,
"Mother,

when I grow up
may I come visit you
if I don't spill talcum
on the bathroom floor

and don't take a shower
with the curtain outside the tub,

if I don't eat muffins in the living room
where the crumbs get on the carpet

and don't use your good stationery
to draw on,

don't try on all the scarves
in your drawer

or the necklaces
in your jewelry box?

May I visit
if I don't leave Magic Marker marks
on the bedspread

or eat tonight's dessert
in the afternoon
or knock over the plant
by the doorway when I come in?

May I visit if I'm careful
to wipe my boots on the mat
when it's raining outside

and to put my umbrella
where it won't drip
all over the floor
and my raincoat too?

May I?
May I visit?"

"Of course," said her mother.
"If you feel like it.

When you're grown up,
please come and visit

because even though you do spill talcum on the floor

bump into plants
track mud on the rug
when you forget to wipe your feet

or any of those things,
it will be fun
to have you then,

just as it is now!"